For Miles — J.O.

For Mia, with love x — L.G.

OXFORD
UNIVERSITY PRESS

Great Clarendon Street, Oxford OX2 6DP

Oxford University Press is a department of the University of Oxford.
It furthers the University's objective of excellence in research, scholarship,
and education by publishing worldwide in

Oxford New York

Auckland Cape Town Dar es Salaam Hong Kong Karachi
Kuala Lumpur Madrid Melbourne Mexico City Nairobi
New Delhi Shanghai Taipei Toronto

With offices in

Argentina Austria Brazil Chile Czech Republic France Greece
Guatemala Hungary Italy Japan Poland Portugal Singapore
South Korea Switzerland Thailand Turkey Ukraine Vietnam

Text copyright © Jan Ormerod 2013
Illustrations copyright © Lindsey Gardiner 2013
The moral rights of the author and artist have been asserted

Database right Oxford University Press (maker)

First published 2013
This edition published in 2013

British Library Cataloguing in Publication Data available

ISBN: 978-0-19–273683-3

3 5 7 9 10 8 6 4 2

Printed in China

Paper used in the production of this book is a natural, recyclable product made
from wood grown in sustainable forests. The manufacturing process conforms
to the environmental regulations of the country of origin

The Wheels on the Bus

Jan Ormerod

Lindsey Gardiner

OXFORD
UNIVERSITY PRESS

The wheels on the bus go round and round,

round and round,

round and round.

The wheels on the bus go round and round,

all day long.

The antelopes

spring so high in the air,

feet off the ground,

jumping all around.

The antelopes **spring** so high in the air, all day long.

Listen to the bell birds ting-a-ling-a-ling,

hear them sing,

tinkle and ring.

Listen to the bell birds ting-a-ling-a-ling, all day long.

The wolfy cubs go 'howl' and 'yowl'.

They 'woo, aroo' and whimper, too.

The wolfy cubs go 'howl' and 'yowl', all day long.

tumble
and
scrap.

Baboons bark
and bounce
all over the bus,
all day long.

The otters in the pool float **paw in paw,**

splash and spray,

pounce and play,

The otters in the pool float paw in paw,

all day long.

The hippos in the mud all **wallow** and **roll**, slump and slide in their watering hole.

The hippos in the mud all wallow and roll,

all day long.

The cheetahs in the grass dash past the bus,

Leaping long, swift and strong.

The cheetahs in the grass dash past the bus, all day long.

The llamas in the field go
trot, trot, trot,
with soft curly hair and their heads in the air.

The llamas in the field go

trot, trot, trot,

all day long.

The sloths move slowly
upside down.

They always smile,

they never frown.

The sloths move slowly **upside down,**

all day long.

The lemurs love to leap from **here** to **there**,

they prance in a group like a dancing troupe!

The lemurs love to leap from **here** to there, all day long.

LDLIFE
PARK

The wheels on the bus

go round and round,

round and round,

round and round.

The wheels on the bus go round and round, **all day long.**